TOURNAMENT

OF

RECKONING

A Fantasy Short Story
BY
ALLIE MARIE

Originally published in the anthology
"Feisty Heroines Romance Collection of Shorts"

A prequel to the
"NETHERBORN SERIES"
By Mike Semloh, coming in winter 2021

TOURNAMENT OF RECKONING

Copyright © 2020 ALLIE MARIE

All rights reserved.

ISBN: 9798709103009

DEDICATION

To my son Mike

CONTENTS

Chapter One   1

Chapter Two   17

Chapter Three   37

CHAPTER ONE
THE DECLARATION

The time had come.

The opportunity for which Siv Anemos had trained her whole life had finally arrived.

With a slight fluttering of nerves, she approached the temple square where a mirrored orb floated. Encircled by a mist of rainbow water droplets, sparks of fire shot from the many octagonal facets covering the sphere.

She smiled at the choice of an instrument of air to

call competitors to the tournament. The fires could die, the waters evaporate, but even without them, the orb would remain floating. Without air, it would fall.

Her last unsettled nerve evaporated as her slightest move sent the mirrored ball bobbing. Air was her strongest element. Even when she did not utilize her powers, a touch of *aerokinesis* always emanated from her being.

The closer she got to the orb, the easier she could see through the shimmer of fire reflecting off the water. Ignoring the armed guards standing in the shadows, she read the names already etched on the facets.

Thirty candidates had entered the competition for the most coveted post in the kingdom of Mesolands—the Grand Sentinel, head of both council and church.

All other council posts were filled through an election process corrupted over the ages. By law, however, the selection of Grand Sentinel was determined by a jousting tournament of all contenders who declared an intent to compete.

Through narrowed eyes, she studied the list, recognizing the names. A number were Necromancers—dragon riders who could touch the four elements of life, death, undeath, and afterlife. More than two dozen Elementalists—practitioners of all the air, earth, water, and fire elements—had signed on. One Medja, a jouster who commanded the single art of water, had etched his name. No Paragon—those able to touch all eight of the elements of magic—had declared.

If ever a playing field had been designed for one individual, this was hers. As a Paragon, she had a distinct advantage, along with her extraordinary jousting.

She spun the ball, rereading the names to be sure.

Yes, she was the lone Paragon—and the only female.

Elation rippled through her, sending the faceted ball dancing. Prejudice and sexism ran rampant in her nation. She'd fought hard for the right to be named as the first female High Priestess in the church.

But as yet, no woman had ever filled a position in the council government, let alone that of the highest ruler.

Seven minutes remained until the deadline. Siv calmed her emotions. She raised her hand, protected by armored metal gloves with an odd assortment of fingers.

Over the eons, she'd created the daunting pair of gauntlets by replacing the normal metal digits with armor scavenged from rivals she'd defeated in jousting tournaments. Each long-pointed appendage sported a different color, size, and shape. Never intended to be of practical use, they served as a stark reminder of her victories to psych out the men she battled. Extending the sharpened claw of a long-defeated Water Elf, she selected a tile with no other names surrounding the space.

As Siv etched her first name on one of the octagonal glass discs, a shadow loomed over her. The fire sparks around the orb burst into flames and nearly dried out the water mist. She spun on her heels and bumped into the massive object behind her.

Rand Emberfang, the hulking Fire Elf from the kingdom of Piironious, steadied her. Even though she was taller than the average Zeph by more than a foot, she still found herself looking into his chest.

"Aren't you a little far from Piironious?" she snapped. She took a step back, bulbous gaze focused on one of Rand's pointed ears. The heat of his touch scorched her to the core—and not because of his command of the fire element.

Rand took a step forward. His eyes darted from side to side, trying to discern where her gaze focused. Her compound eyes could be looking anywhere, but his masculine hubris decided she was looking at his crotch.

With a subtle breath, she blew cold air between them. She lowered the temperature a bit with another blast, satisfied when a shiver overtook the Fire Elf.

Her hair matched the exact same vibrant shade of white as Rand's, but where her skin was pale almost to the point of translucent blue, his burned the deep volcanic red of fire. They had crossed paths at many of the same jousting events. His renowned jousting skills equaled Siv's, but they had never faced off in a competition. Their social interactions, however infrequent because of schedules and distance, always provided interesting opportunities to flirt and scope each other out.

Siv had always known that, like oil and vinegar, Fire Elves and Zephs didn't mix. As a species, Fire Elves commanded awe and respect unparalleled in any realm—fierce warriors who yearned for a glorious death as their legacy. They had no trouble engaging in sex with any members of the other kingdoms, but when it came time to settle and have offspring, they usually mated with one of their own.

She drew to her full height, still a half-head shorter than Rand. Tilting her head back, she said, "Now, if you'll excuse me, I have to finalize my signature. There's less than a minute to go."

"You certainly waited until the last minute, didn't you?" Rand moved closer to Siv, peering over her head as she etched her last name on a tile amongst the blank octagonal tiles surrounding it.

"I did." Siv finished and pushed past Rand.

"Not quite." With seconds to spare, he reached through the mist and fire. A bolt of flame shot from his finger, inscribing his name on the mirrored tile to the right of her signature.

"What are you doing?" Siv demanded.

As he withdrew his hand, the fire and mist diminished. A shroud of unbreakable glass surrounded the darkened sphere. Soldiers emerged from the shadows to retrieve the sphere for delivery to the Council Chambers.

***

Council members milled around a refreshment table, engaging in small talk as they awaited delivery of the mirror. Across the room, a portly Zeph caught the attention of a lanky colleague. He inclined his head toward the chamber room. Both men slipped beyond the doors and headed toward the huge round table centered on the floor of the circular room. Twelve unusual saddle chairs surrounded the polished metal round table. Each saddle bore the name of a champion jouster and his or her retired dragon.

Gallery-style seating lined the walls. Reserved for spectators during public meetings, the chairs sat empty for the closed-door meeting about to begin.

Tudoriax, the Senior Delegate and longest-reigning member, chose a golden saddle with the names etched across the sides. He mounted with pompous dignity, plopping his large posterior in the groove. His feet slipped from the stirrups, nearly unseating him in the process. A quick clutch on the pummel prevented an undignified fall to the ground.

"It's good that we do not have to rely on your jousting skills to settle the concerns of Mesolands, Tudoriax. Or should I say your lack thereof?" mocked Zelman Maxir, Secretary of Internal Affairs. He opted for a blood-red saddle decorated with iridescent dragon scales.

"Which none of *us* have," retorted an angry Tudoriax. He slithered from the golden saddle and scrutinized the remaining empty seats.

None of the current council members had earned their seats by winning the jousting competition. The tournaments had been suspended after a plague struck and nearly wiped out the Mesolands dragons. For several generations there were not enough grown creatures to allow for the jousting tournaments to determine the new members. Soon, the process evolved into candidates declaring for the empty seats, won by purchased votes and outright deceit, until all members had been voted into their positions rather than earning the spot.

As a result, corruption became the standard and members served so long that the newer generations never had the chance to compete—or even campaign—for positions.

Retirement was mandatory at the age of two hundred. But without notice, the Grand Sentinel had taken early retirement and immigrated to a new post in the Northern Realm, catching the council off guard.

Tudoriax settled on a polished bronze saddle bearing the name of Siv Anemos and her latest retired dragon, Ordan.

"Tudoriax, can we not just hold an election?" Zelman asked. "Or can you not simply name yourself as the new ruler?"

The senior councilman shook his head. "I've checked this thoroughly with the Judiciary Office. It is law. If we'd known sooner, we could have eliminated the jousting competition from the rules and held an election. But we did not know in time to change the Grand Sentinel to the elected posts. We're committed to the decrees in place. A tournament must be held to name the new ruler."

"Are proper strategies in place to ensure the outcome, Tudoriax?"

"Only preliminary so far, Zelman. Once we see who will compete, we'll finalize plans."

The two men ended the covert conversation as council members filed in and took seats.

The Senior Delegate banged a gavel made of humanoid bones shaped like a fist to call the meeting to order.

Two pairs of armed guards formed a square and entered the ceremonial chambers, flanking the now-darkened mirrored orb floating between them. After a ceremonial circle around the roundtable, the sentries stopped at Tudoriax's seat.

The Senior Delegate took the sphere from the air and set it on the table. With a push of his palms, he flattened the ball into a sheet of tiles. He slid the squares toward the Minister of Internal Affairs, who began sorting names into columns.

With a dismissive wave of his pudgy fingers, Tudoriax sent the four sentinels on their way. In unison, they did an about-face and marched in the opposite direction to complete a circle around the table before they exited the council doors. The last two turned to bow and then closed the doors behind them.

The council remained quiet for a full minute, broken at last when Tudoriax gave the bone gavel a sharp rap.

Secretariat Rhymer Faticus pulled one of his cylindrical metal cuffs from his sleeves, ready to etch minutes of the meeting.

After greeting his colleagues, Tudoriax stood and said, "We're required to hold a joust to select a new ruler. This is an elimination competition, not a deathmatch. How many rounds occur will depend on how many entrants apply. In the preliminaries, competitors are paired in match-ups. The winner of each goes on to the next round, while the loser is eliminated from further competition. In the next round, those winners square off another series of matches, and so on, until the final elimination match-up. That winner becomes tournament champion—and the Grand Sentinel of Mesolands."

"Does anyone remember how competitions were conducted?" Rhymer asked, peering into a scrying stone on his ring to look for records. "We've not had multi-round tournaments for eons. Most of the jousts we have now are to settle disputes between farmers whose stock has strayed over the line, or to determine who has the right to elements on a property. Even some of our very minor skirmishes have left someone dead over a petty difference. Think of the fervor with stakes as high as these."

Zelman slapped his hands on the flattened mirror tiles. "I've perused the list. Thirty-two contenders have declared. There are twenty-four Elementalists, nine Necromancers, and one Medja. And two Paragons. Before we do anything else, we should take into consideration these Paragons, our two most troublesome contenders."

"Yes?"

"One is a Fire Elf. Rand Emberfang, Tudoriax." Zelman winced as he glanced at the tiles.

Tudoriax leaned forward, the rest of the council following suit. "From Piironious? How can someone from another kingdom enter?" His voice thundered.

Rhymer twirled his cuffs to find the appropriate etchings in his records and shrugged. "A costly loophole that is out of our hands. Another obscure rule from the ancient past allows anyone from the eight kingdoms to enter our tournament if they have a challenge with one of our citizens. I know this Fire Elf, and he will be a threat. Who is the other

Paragon?"

Zelman cleared his throat. "Um…"

"Speak up, fool!"

"It is—Lady Siv Anemos, the High Priestess."

Anger surged through Tudoriax until his pale skin turned purple. "Siv, the Tempest of Mesolands? Our 'Feisty Troublemaker?'" He shouted the nicknames with such vengeance that spittle sprayed from his lips. He wiped his mouth with the back of his hand, then held both arms to the side to maintain his balance on the saddle.

A few snickers rose from the other council members but abated quickly as the Senior Delegate glared.

"When this tournament is over, she will get her just rewards. She's nothing but trouble. Here is what I think of the Tempest of Mesolands." He rocked his hips on Siv's retired saddle, grinding down. He wrapped his fingers around the pommel. With a lewd leer, he jerked his hand up and down in a suggestive manner.

Laughter burst forth until Tudoriax reached for the gavel and pounded. He leaned his girth forward in the saddle.

"She cannot win," he said. "This meeting is called to order."

Zelman continued. "She's the most skilled dragon rider in Mesolands and commands all the arts. Rand is the best from Piironious, and despite the loophole to enter, he can never attain the position. Chances are quite likely that he and Siv will face each other in the final competition. We can control the process by declaring that only one magical power shall be used during each stage of the competition."

"If Rand follows the path of his comrades who like to die a glorious death, he may meet that desired fate while fighting Siv, and we'll be rid of his interference once and for all. But if Rand wins, Siv is eliminated and since he cannot take the position, we will select one ourselves."

"And if she wins?" Rhymer's tone was insistent.

Zelman gave an exasperated shake of the head,

then said, "As the Senior Delegate Tudoriax has already said, she cannot win."

Murmurs rippled around the table as council members reacted.

The Senior Delegate banged the gavel to silence the room.

"We have thirty-two hours before the challengers assemble. I suggest we begin our strategy."

CHAPTER TWO

THE BONDING

"What! You're wearing *that?*" asked an incredulous Nyrin. The pixie fluttered her wings to rise upward so that she could make eye contact with her taller friend.

"I am." Siv gave a defiant shrug that sent her white-silver hair billowing.

"But, Lady Siv…" Despite their years of

friendship, Nyrin often addressed the High Priestess by her noble title.

"As the rules of our church decree, I'm covered from neck to toe. They don't specify what constitutes a covering." Siv unfolded the incandescent wings on her back and drifted to the ceiling. She twirled in a full circle, her delicate clothing shimmering with each move.

Nyrin laughed. "Yes, you are indeed covered, *as decreed*, but it's…transparent. The men will have a hard time focusing."

"Their problem, not mine." Siv's continued to float. With her command over air, she could add grace to any movement. Her armor was indeed translucent, save for the strategically-placed crystals covering her private parts

"And the males may look all they will, but these crystals can never fail and reveal what they protect. But I'll also admit, I have a complete bodysuit under the sheer material. The translucency is intentional and serves my purpose." Siv would not admit out loud that the translucency served to distract the males who only objectified women. She also intended to the opportunity to rebel against the government decree requiring women to be covered from neck to toe at all public events. A ridiculous decree in her opinion, considering that the form-fitting clothing of both male and female citizens left little to the imagination.

The only other solid material Siv wore were the rings on each of her ten fingers, representing the dragons that had served her in battle. While most jousters bonded with one dragon until death, a few had seen service with two or more. Siv was the lone Mesolander who had bonded ten times before. Such a fact might convey to an outsider many poor dragons had bonded to a losing jouster. In reality, Siv was acquiring her eleventh dragon because she was the best of the best, outlasting the loyal creatures that served her.

"This material is incredibly lustrous." Nyrin reached to touch one of Siv's arms. The sheer sleeve immediately changed to metallic mail. The pixie jumped in surprise. With a rapid sweep of her other arm, she raked her fingernails across Siv's stomach.

Before the tips could touch the fabric, her fingernails tapped against the metal chain as it formed.

She stared in disbelief. After a few seconds, the armor covering Siv's stomach returned to the original shimmery sheer material.

"What just happened?" Nyrin asked. "Where did the armor come from?"

"I've been working on this for eons with Livanth, the alchemist. I had the idea but not the knowledge to create a see-through fabric that could be converted to armor. You should've seen some of the disastrous results before she discovered what would work."

"No one's seen this in competition yet?" Nyrin asked.

Siv shook her head. "No."

Moving in slow motion, Nyrin raised her hand to give a gentle poke to Siv's collarbone, but once again, before she could make contact, the filmy fabric gorget near the jouster's neck changed to the life-protecting shield.

"It's amazing, Siv. But jousts take all of six to

eight seconds for two riders to pass each other. Will your suit become armor quick enough to protect you from a lance or sword? Will it protect your wings?"

"Here, I'll show you." Siv tossed a sword to Nyrin. The nimble air sprite sprang upward and twisted gracefully, catching the handle. Despite her diminutive size, she was capable of lifting one hundred times her weight. Hefting the heavy weapon above her head, she drifted downward until her feet touched the ground.

"Come at me, like you are attacking," Siv demanded.

"Oh, no, no." Nyrin shook her head. "I'm a flight guard, not a jouster. My job is to guide you through the air."

"Hey, flight guards have to stave off attacks after their jousters become unseated, you know." Siv unsheathed her majestic sword and sliced through the air. Ominous metallic vibrations resonated with her every swoosh.

Nyrin backed up. "Not me. I know how to shift

through the battle to guide you, but not how to fight."

Siv rolled her rounded eyes, then stared.

Nyrin huffed and made lack-luster crosses with the sword.

"Lunge, Nyrin!" Siv commanded.

The pixie readied her position, aimed for Siv's upper arm, and clamped her eyes shut. Wings flapping fiercely, she swung the blade with all her might and steeled for the impact of sword on armor—or the resulting cry of pain from her mentor.

"Ayyyy!"

The shriek came—not from Siv, but from Nyrin, As the effect of metal meeting metal rippled through her body, she dropped the sword and opened her eyes.

Siv stood before her, swathed in full armor, wings outstretched, unscathed by the attack. Seconds later, the chainmail returned to the sheer clothing.

Nyrin shook her head. "You nearly rattled my brains out of my head. I've never seen anything so incredible."

Siv nodded. "I can turn my full armor on at will, or the suit forms an automatic shield if it senses the approach of danger."

"As long as your gems cover your jewels, there is little danger." Nyrin giggled. "I wonder what Rand will think when he sees you."

Siv narrowed her eyes at the name of her chief competitor. "He shouldn't be allowed to compete. He's not even from Mesolands. How can he become Grand Sentinel?"

"It's because of some obscure rule. Someone from another kingdom can enter if he is involved in a complaint with another entrant. I'm sure you will face him in the final match. And we all know that the most important goal to a Fire Elf is to die a glorious death."

"Which I can give him." Siv shoved her sword into its sheath.

"And may you be the champion of this year's competition, Siv," Nyrin said with a bow.

"Mark my words, Nyrin. I *shall* be this year's champion and the first female Grand Sentinel of the Council Chambers. It's time to free Mesolands from the corruption and bias incorporated by our ruling males."

Siv's hair turned to a stormy silver as fiery air turmoiled around her head. Her eyes focused on some object indeterminable to Nyrin. With a flex of her shoulders, the Zeph's expansive wings opened to their full width and breadth.

With another shrug, Siv retracted her wings. She grabbed a long cloak and tossed it over her shoulders. She picked up her lance, made of the special green metal known as Havenium, which allowed memories to be stored in the spear. Each jouster had a similar weapon that remembered its every move from previous tournaments.

She faced Nyrin. "Meet me in the stables." Swiveling on one foot, she stormed toward the door, gale-force winds whirling around her.

***

Along the walls of the rounded Council Chambers, workers prepared the elevated seats for V.I.P. spectators. A solid black line a foot wide cut the room in half, running across the floor and over the top of the mighty Round Table, down to the floor on the other side, dividing the bleachers. Two female Zephs in apprentice jouster suits polished the saddle seats. The backless chairs had stirrups to help the council members maintain balance, and on one side or the other had cradles that once held the lances of the dragon riders.

"Esrala, look." The taller of the two lowered her voice in awe in front of one seat. "This saddle once belonged to Lady Siv's last dragon."

"Let me polish it, Giln." Esrala floated in excitement as she neared the saddle.

"I was here first." Giln trailed her palms over the hide, fingers touching the etchings that identified the former rider and dragon as Siv and Brank.

"Well, you're done so it's my turn. Lady Siv is my all-time idol." Esrala rubbed the leather with the same reverence.

"Mine too." Giln sighed with anticipation. "Do you realize that if she wins the competition today, she'll be the first female to not only have earned a spot on the High Council, but to become Grand Sentinel? That means she'll represent Mesolands at the coronation of Elira as the first *Ortu Saad* in Paragonia. Imagine, our first female ruler attending the coronation of another first female ruler. What times we live in."

"Have you heard the rumors that Elira was in her last stages of pregnancy when she fought demons in a battle, and that her son Argon was born on the footsteps of the Netherworld?"

"I heard she had one foot in the Netherworld and one at the Gateway, so her son could have been born either demon or angel. Siv is as brave as Elira is."

"Yes. I'm so excited. Siv will win. *She must* win. For all the progress this council claims to make, they still cast females as insignificant members of society. Lady

Siv will win her place and make things right."

"They'll fight dirty to do everything they can to prevent her from winning."

"But, she's the shrewdest competitor, has the best record, and her new dragon was a prized hatchling of her best dragon. They're a force to which no others can compare."

"She will win," Esrala repeated. "Let's finish so we can watch history in the making."

Before heading back to the task at hand, the two pixies raised their right hands and tapped the tips of their first and middle fingers together three times—for the luck of all the females of Mesolands.

***

Tightening the cloak around her, Siv made her way through the long corridor of the stables. Most of the stalls were empty, as riders had already claimed their dragons and reported to the staging area.

Sporadic whirls of small dust dervishes sent loose straw and grass into her path as the cleaning imps did their chores. Nasty but necessary, the green-skinned creatures worked to keep the stables and animals free of vermin and crud. The dirtier the task, the more the ill-tempered creatures enjoyed their work.

She stopped at the last stall. An iridescent ball of scales with limbs nestled on a pile of straw. Two gnarly imps were cleaning the beast's rainbow-like scales.

One shriveled Pica imp, sporting wild tufts of maroon hair over his body, balanced on the dragon's back, using a long-handled brush to scrub along the dragon's elongated graceful neck.

The other, a gray-haired Pica imp layered in wrinkles, used the hollowed-out talon of a long-dead dragon to cover his fist. He scraped under the flexible but steel-hard scales.

"Yum," he said as he scooped a film of crust and mites. He stuck the talon in his mouth and sucked it clean. "They pays us in apples, but me would do it for free for all these tasty treats."

"Get out of here, you disgusting reprobate." Nyrin buzzed the grizzled imp, hovering with angry wings flapping. "Go away! Get!"

"Hey, me not done here." He reached up to try to peek under Nyrin's tunic.

"Yes, you are." Siv raised her pinky and shot a spark of fire at the offender's butt.

"Yeeouch!" The imp danced a jig while fanning his behind. He farted, fueling the spark with a bit more energy than desired.

"Begone, you two heathens." Siv tossed apples from a barrel. The maroon-headed one caught the fruits as fast as she threw them and darted out the door. She turned and caught the grizzled gray using the talon to lift her cloak. She wiggled her pinky finger again and sent a bolt that looped around and struck the imp's other butt cheek. He danced his way behind his comrade, his noxious gasses keeping the spark dancing.

Nyrin held her nose as she fanned her wings.

"Will you go after him and send him a healing

zap?" Siv asked.

"Oh, must I?"

"Yes, please."

Grumbling, Nyrin held her nose and flew after the offending scamp.

"How are you, Ghymugras?" Siv turned to her animal and cooed. The wyvern, a two-legged dragon with a barbed tail, was the first female Siv had trained, and her first Paragon dragon, gifted as Siv was with all eight arts. The creature unfurled her wings. Despite her massive size, she fluttered like a feather in the wind and lowered her long neck to nuzzle Siv's neck.

"I'm fine, Lady Siv." The words came out in a melodic chiming, echoing in the air with a delicateness unexpected from a creature so large. Ghymugras, whose cumbersome name meant "Dragon of the Air," could speak, a rare gift bestowed upon her when she was a baby. Wyverns could usually only communicate with their riders through mental dialogue.

"Do I detect a quiver of nerves, Ghy?" Siv ran her

knuckles gently along the wyvern's jawline.

The nickname soothed the worried creature. "Maybe a little. They told me we will fail, my Lady."

"Who did?"

"The other dragons. And their riders. Even some of the females have teased me, telling me I will die because you are my rider and you have already bonded with ten before me."

"You will not die, Ghy. Did we not train every day since I selected you? Have we not taken on jousters of all ranks in our sessions, and were we not the victors in the end? None of my dragons were killed in jousts, I just outlasted them. So, no, you will not die, but I may wear you out and then you will join the others in the retirement circle someday."

"This is your most important of all tournaments, and I fear I am not worthy of you. There were so many other more experienced dragons you should have chosen."

"That is true," Siv said. She smiled at the slight stiffening of her ride. "Yet you are here precisely *because* I chose you. I wanted only the best and you are the best."

Ghy visibly relaxed and closed her eyes, her lashes stroking Siv's cheek as she nuzzled again.

"I have something for you," Siv whispered. She pushed up the sleeve of her cloak, and removed a bracelet-like adornment that matched the ring on her right hand.

"My bonding ring!" The dragon flexed her talons and allowed Siv to slide the bracelet over one, equating its placement on the dragon to the ring on her humanoid hand.

Dragon and rider extended their limbs to admire the matching oval stones that were more than adornment. Cut from the same diamond, the two gems held a power that would bind Siv to her wyvern, to connect their thoughts and movements during jousts, and in all aspects of their rapport. By the magical attuning of a matching ring worn by both rider and dragon, the pair were now bonded telepathically.

Siv lifted the gorget at her neck to reveal a necklace with ten other rings. "These are the rings of your predecessors. Like the metal shaft of my lance, they hold memories of my competitions. Whenever we joust, these rings will be embedded in the handle of my lance, and through them, their magical memories will guide us."

"I am honored, my Lady. I will do my best to honor you and my predecessors." Her sensors signaled another presence, which she ignored. Her unique eyes already knew who had arrived.

In the far doorway, Rand Emberfang leaned against the frame, watching Siv's bonding. Not only was her new dragon an impressive creature, but the Zeph herself was. Taller than most females of her kingdom, her every move exuded grace and fluidity, with air her strongest element. He'd long been attracted to her.

Although they had never jousted against each other, Rand had seen many of her matches and knew her to be a formidable opponent. They'd engaged in flirtatious encounters off the field before, but this tournament would give him the opportunity to get to know her more—and likely he'd challenge her in the final match.

He took long, quiet strides, enjoying the melodious blend of Siv's calm voice mixing with the blue wyvern's tinkling notes. As he moved closer, however, the chiming syllables turned into a roar as the dragon raised her head and blew out a fireless blast of hot air, knocking Rand flat on his back.

"Good girl, Ghy," Siv praised, stroking the beast's neck. She smirked over her shoulder. "I would think you knew better than to disrupt a rider bonding with her dragon, Rand. Be glad we were finished. She could sense you were not a threat to me, or you may have been fried to a crisp."

Rand bounced to his feet, a slight look of shock on his face. "How did you know I was here?" He rolled his eyes skyward and added, "I forgot about those all-seeing eyes of yours."

"I saw you the moment you arrived." Siv declined to mention that she had also felt the heat of his presence when he stepped to the open door. She had tamped down her power of air, allowing her own command of fire to blend with Rand's so that he had no knowledge she was even aware of him.

He took a few steps forward.

Siv whirled on him. Ghymugras gave a warning snort, a puff of smoke escaping her nostrils. "Why are you here, Rand, in this tournament in my kingdom? They will never name you the Grand Sentinel."

He shrugged. With a cautious hand, he reached to stroke the dragon's long neck. "She's already prepared to defend you to the death, isn't she? She's a beauty—like her rider."

"Spare me." She elbowed the Fire Elf from her path. "Leave me alone, Rand, I have a tournament to win."

"I think I might have something to say about that," he said, moving behind her as she reached for a bridle. He wrapped his arms around her and drew her to him.

Siv hitched her breath, taking in the slightly smokey scent of Rand, aware of his strength, his essence—and of a firm pressure on her lower back.

Either her armor had activated under her cloak to protect her from Rand—or his body had activated of its own accord.

CHAPTER THREE
THE RECKONING

Siv took a deep breath at the entrance to the waiting room, where candidates for the tournament gathered before they were granted access to the council. With a deep breath, she flung the cloak aside and pushed open the massive double doors.

Small clusters of contenders dotted the room. Siv's eyes focused straight ahead, but with her ability to see in all directions, she noticed the gaping jaws and wide-eyed stares of the males. For just a moment, a flutter of nerves invaded as she endured the gawks and murmurs. With a deliberate but imperceptible summoning of the power of air, she set the delicate materials flowing, crystals maintaining their designated places. One jouster tripped over his own feet. Another dropped his lance. As he bent to pick it up, he bumped into another, sending a row of males toppling.

First mission accomplished. Siv relaxed. *I've got this.*

The gong signaled the warning to fall into formation, and the jousters scrambled to line up.

A warm breath danced along her gorget and Rand's voice whispered in her ear, "What a nice surprise. How pleased I'll be when we march." He leaned closer. "I'll have a most delightful view of your—crystals."

In response, Siv unfolded her wings to their full glory, pushing Rand to the side. With a flick of her wrist, she hefted her shield and lance. Her gaze swept over the other weapons. Every lance was fitted with blunted padding called a coronal in place of a pointed tip, but the shaft could still break off and pierce armor.

Ahead of the competitors, sentries pushed open the large doors leading to the council chambers. Two directed the jousters to walk in single file toward the council table, sending half to the right side of the black strip dividing the room. The remaining competitors would fill the left half.

As Siv entered, murmurs increased to waves of sound that crashed into a crescendo of shouts and clapping as more spectators became aware of her clothing.

Because of her wingspan, she had more room on either side of her than many of the other contenders. She struck a stoic pose, feet planted apart, one arm holding her shield chest-high, the other holding her lance.

Standing at the podium, the Secretariat began the tedious process of his welcome address, announcing names of the important guests and spectators, then the thirty-two competitors.

As the ancient secretary droned on, Siv scanned around her without moving her head. Many jousters stood as motionless as she, while others fidgeted. Who her opponents would be depended on the results of the other match-ups. She'd seen tournaments where an unexpected rival beat champions because of sheer hubris.

She noted five potential threats, including the usurping contender from Piironious. It would be a pity if she and Rand were paired in the first match. She aimed her gaze to her right. The red Fire Elf stood out among the pale blue skins of the Mesolanders, in skin tone and size. He was a worthy opponent and for a moment she wondered if she would think less of him if she were to beat him in the tournament.

She cleared that thought immediately and shut down her hormones to concentrate on the task at hand. The Minister of Internal Affairs stood to read the rules.

"Thirty-two names have been etched on the Sphere of Intent. Contenders will be paired at random for the first round and will compete in an elimination match. Riders will charge each other, pass, make a U-turn at the opposing end and charge again. Riders will make up to three passes to determine a winner of the match. Each winner will then go on to the next round. The last two remaining contenders shall face-off in the final match-up.

"The rules are simple. The winner of each match-up shall be determined by any one of the following incidences, whichever occurs first.

"Rule One: This is not a battle to the death, but an elimination match. A rider whose lance breaks or imbeds in the armor of an opponent is considered to have dealt a deadly blow and deemed the winner.

"Rule Two: A rider who causes another opponent to become unseated *and* to fall off his mount, whether or not the fallen rider lives or dies, is declared the winner.

"Rule Three: A rider whose lance pierces the armor of an opponent, whether or not the opponent lives or dies, is declared the winner.

"Rule Four: The failure of any of these events to occur in the match will result in a draw and those contenders will go on to the next round.

"Rule Five: Competitors may invoke any of the elemental arts: air, fire, water, earth, or necromance: life, death, undeath, afterlife. However, The Council will declare one magic art as exempt during each round. No rider may utilize the art that has been exempted. The art of water has been disallowed in the first round."

The Secretariat introduced the Senior Delegate and then called Tudoriax to the podium.

"Are you ready?" the Senior Delegate asked the jousters.

Nods and affirmative responses signaled a unanimous response.

"The tournament to select the new Grand Sentinel of Mesolands is now open. Riders, report to the staging areas." Tudoriax slammed the bone gavel on the podium.

Tremors shook the stadium, startling several

jousters. Quakes continued. The black stripe dividing the room began to split. The round chambers fanned out in two equal halves that swiveled on a turntable mechanism underneath. The wall disconnected at the stripe, opening onto the great outdoor arena where the waiting citizenry of Mesolands filled the seats. Cheers arose as the two half-rounds locked into place opposite the grandstands and the dignitaries faced the ordinary citizens of Mesolands.

At each end, huge projection screens floated, soon to light up with the names of the contenders for each match. Huge doors beneath the screens hid the rider, dragon and their flight guard who would enter the arena when called forward.

Though the tournament area—known as the list field—was groomed for a ground competition, this event would be conducted in the air. As Mesolands was a floating plane, the stadium was constructed with a moveable bottom which opened to the galaxy.

Daylight brightened the sky above, the dark universe stretched below as the field slid open to reveal the endless void into which many an unseated jouster had fallen. Some were rescued by their dragons, others by use of one of the arts. Some disappeared forever.

Sixteen contenders filed downstairs to the East Stage, Siv and the fifteen males in her group to the West Stage. As they passed through the doors leading to the staging area, an apprentice jouster handed out darkened red crystals. Resembling scrying stones, the chips would glow and reveal the rider's number moments before that match was to begin.

Siv folded her wings to get past the archway, and the male Zeph before her turned abruptly. She nearly ran into him.

"You're not going to win, Siv." Dakrus Orkon leaned in with a leer and dropped his gaze. "You think you can distract us with your gauntlets bearing trophies from your past conquests. Or with your clever costume." He aimed his finger to jab Siv's chest. Before the tip touched her, a fist-sized section of spiked armor clamped on his finger and he let out a yell.

"Let me go, let me go."

At her will, the metal slowly released his fingertip, leaving scratches but no bleeding—this time.

"What kind of dark arts magic are you using?" Dakrus asked as he shook his hand.

In response, Siv poked his chest with her forefinger. "I suggest you keep that digit—or any of your appendages—to yourself before it becomes the next finger on my gauntlet."

Before Dakrus could answer, the giant floating monitors in the staging area lit up. One showed the pending scoreboard, while another showed the arena as scrying drones panned the crowds.

A sentry entered the area and shouted, "Inspections!"

The competitors formed a line, holding shields up and lances to their sides. Examiners scrutinized every weapon to ensure that the sharp tips for battle had been replaced with blunted coronals.

A piercing vibration permeated the air and a jouster held up his crystal. The number "1" blazed gold.

"I'm first!" He stepped into the passageway to wait for his flight guard to lead his dragon to the gates. As soon as he mounted, he raised his lance to signify his readiness. The doors parted and the team soared into the arena to face its competition on the list field. A modest chorus of cheers broke out.

"It's always better to get it over with early in the elimination rounds, isn't it?" Rand's warm breath brushed her cheeks as he leaned closer to her.

"Is it?"

"If I touch your shoulder, will your armor chomp my finger like it did Dakrus?"

Siv turned. "Why don't you try it and see, Rand?"

The Fire Elf narrowed his eyes, then shook his head. "Now is not the time. I'd like to know more about this armor later. But how can you wear something so sheer and revealing, yet it can turn to the sturdiest of metal? Is it allowed?"

"It's never been worn in a tournament before, so I doubt it is disallowed. But as I'm bound by the rules of being covered from neck to toe, *I* am perfectly legal."

"Lethal is more like it," Rand said with a wink.

Groans rose from the group. Siv turned to the monitor in time to see the competitor from their group struck by his opponent's lance. The blow unseated him, but his tether prevented him from falling into the void. The dragon swooped low and extended his tail to push the rider back into the saddle. The winning team took a victory lap as the losers sailed to the sidelines for treatment. The scrying drone zoomed in on the rider's arm, dislocated by the violent clash.

"Oh." Siv winced. Match 1 was over.

"Fifteen more to go," someone shouted.

One by one, Siv's competitors answered the call of their crystal, until she was the last rider in the room. Several riders from her group had already joined the first rider on the eliminated side. Rand and Dakrus had easily dispatched their opponents on the first pass.

She wondered if the matches were truly random,

but if the council had tried to sway the outcome of Siv's competition by making her wait until last, they had failed.

Unstressed by the delay, she had studied the matches on the big screen, assessing the skills of the winners. Her crystal squelched and glowed red.

Round 16 was about to begin.

She entered the hallway, where Nyrin and Ghy hovered.

"It's about time they called us," the flight guard grumbled. She turned the reins over to Siv, who leapt into the saddle. She extended the lance to full length and ensured it was locked in place.

"Ghy, are you ready?"

"I am."

"Nyrin?"

"Ready."

"Wings out."

Each extended their wings to full span, and rose on the air. As soon as the gates opened, Siv and Ghy, guided by Nyrin, flew to the starting line, met by cheers and claps.

The opposing team entered from the other gate, but instead of settling at the starting line, the flight guard led the riding duo in a series of flips and somersaults before they landed in place.

Cheers broke out louder than Siv's team had received.

"Should we respond?" Ghy asked in her melodic tone.

"Not now, girl. We'll have our moment to showboat." Siv patted her mount's neck.

Nyrin buzzed with energy as she motioned for the animal to place her feet on the starting mark. Once in place, Siv steadied the lance upright.

The showboating team flipped again and flew into position. The opponent raised his lance.

At the signal to charge, Siv lowered the lance, balancing the unwieldy weight by tucking the base under her right armpit and aiming the point to the left of the dragon's head. Ghy shot forward and increased speed. Siv's rounded eyes gave her an advantage of seeing distance and closeup. She noted her opponent's glance drift toward the crystals shifting across her breasts.

When his gaze returned to the task at hand, it was just in time to see Siv's coronal aimed at his chest. His eyes widened as her lance caught him under the breastplate and lifted him out of his saddle. He jerked over the back and tail of his mount, with only his tether keeping him from falling into the void.

And just like that, Match 16 was over.

"Is this our moment?" Ghy asked.

"It is indeed." With that, Siv nudged her dragon into a backward somersault to the delight of the spectators and guided her toward their gate.

The umpire signaled that Siv won the match-up. Her face appeared on the monitors.

Thunderous cheers rumbled from the civilian spectators.

Council members sat in stony silence with arms crossed.

The crowd quieted, waiting for Tudoriax to declare the winner. He rose and paused. Finally, he extended his arm toward her in acknowledgment.

The civilian side of the stadium erupted in more cheers, rocking as thousands and thousands of spectators stamped their feet in approval.

Nyrin circled and landed on Ghy's head, then knelt to kiss the thick hide. She then skied down the neck toward Siv. She grinned. With wings fluttering at full speed, she levitated and flew to kiss Siv's forehead.

Siv smiled, then clapped her hands. "Calm down, girls, we still have a long way to go." The trio entered the gateway, the heavy doors closing on but not muffling the thunderous applause.

A tight-jawed Tudoriax sat and heaved a deep breath. He angled his head toward one of the sentries and gave a slight nod. The sentry responded by tapping the butt of his lance on the floor twice.

***

The second and third rounds saw the elimination of more competitors. Matches grew more intense, and injuries more severe. The arts clashed, resulting in lightning, fireworks, smokescreens, death masks, rain, and more. Siv's skills proved so strong, however, she'd required no magic.

Siv, Rand, and Dakrus from the West Stage had easily dispatched their opponents in their quarter-finals. Only one team remained from the East Stage. The head umpire called the four finalists to the center of the jousting field.

The head umpire announced, "Congratulations on making it to the semi-finals. With three teams from the West Stage and one from the East, we must balance the competition. One team will move from West to East. Your scrying stones will alert you to which area you will report. You'll have one hour to have a meal and prepare for your next match. Good luck."

Piercing whines echoed with humming as the stones vibrated in the jousters' hands. Siv glanced at her stone until "EAST" appeared in gold letters against the red surface.

Dakrus headed back to the West Stage. As he passed Siv, he shouted, "Looks like you're heading to the losing side, Siv."

Ghy stiffened as Dakrus' mount snorted a puff of black smoke shaped like a death dragon into her path. The wyvern blew billows of white smoke drawn from her powers of life, smashing the offending dragon against the wall. With little effort, Siv blasted air through clenched teeth to dissipate the dark cloud, forcing Dakrus to grab the pommel to remain in his seat.

Her power of air was far greater than the Necromancer's command of the death element he'd just displayed.

She patted Ghy's neck. Nyrin looped head over heels and stretched out her arm to stroke the dragon's cheek as they flew to their new location.

Siv said, "We've just had minor skirmishes so far, ladies. Now we face a battle I cannot lose."

***

As spectators rushed to concession stands, the council gathered in their private wing, where a feast awaited them.

Zelman huddled with the Senior Delegate. "Siv is among the best of the best, Tudoriax. Her skills are definitely in the top three of our four finalists"

"Siv will joust either Rand or Dakrus in this match." Tudoriax reached for a glass of wine. "Things are in our favor. Either is formidable enough to take her out. If she fights Dakrus first, we've put some insurances in place to handicap her. Should she make it to the finals, she'll be near exhaustion when she faces Rand."

Zelman rolled his eyes. "Fire Elves are the most feared race when it comes to fighting. You know the saying: 'If a Fire Elf steps on your foot, *you* apologize first.' They've been on the frontlines of every battle since Prima Morda and they live to die a glorious death. What if Rand wins the final?"

"Who cares, Zelman?" Tudoriax snapped. With a clap of his hands, a mist appeared and spun before him. It dissolved, leaving an ancient leather-bound record floating in its wake. He wagged his fingers and metal pages flipped until he stilled his hand. "According to the Etchings of Law, his entry was a fluke that could not be prevented. But he can't be Grand Sentinel because he's not Mesolands-born. That is ironclad. The end."

"Would it matter if Siv becomes the Grand Sentinel?" Zelman asked. "She is as worthy as any competitor we've seen and is fully capa…"

Cold silence met the minister's statement. He opened his mouth and then clamped shut, realizing he may have just sealed his death warrant.

***

Siv tended to her dragon before taking a break. Esrala and Giln, the female apprentice jousters, struggled to carry a metal tub to the staging area. They set it before Siv, busy inspecting her dragon's claws.

She stood. Although older, she was as lithe as the others. Only when she removed the dead sheep from the tub and tossed the carcass to Ghymugras did her true strength become evident. Both trainees stepped back in awe.

"Take your time and enjoy, Ghy," she crooned. "Esrala and Giln, where are the imps who should be attending to my dragon?"

The younger females shook their heads. "We haven't seen them."

Nyrin fluttered into the hallway. "Lady Siv, you need to come eat. Your food is ready."

"I'm coming." She rubbed the dragon's snort and turned to the apprentices. "Please take care of her. Only allow her to drink a small tub of water, please."

"Yes, Lady Siv." The apprentices scampered from the room to do her bidding.

As Siv walked toward the West Stage dining hall, she glanced at the countdown on the time monitor. Twenty minutes. Food was the last thing on her mind but she needed the sustenance. She joined Nyrin at a small table to one side. A server brought her a plate stacked with fruits and breads.

Across the room, the other jouster finished his meal and leaned back in the chair. He nodded once and Siv returned the greeting. His name was Altin and they had trained together when they were young, but never jousted in the same competition.

She nibbled on a hunk of bread, leaving Altin alone to his thoughts.

"Aren't you hungry, Siv?" Nyrin popped a grape in her mouth. "You aren't nervous, are you?"

"No, to tell you the truth, I'm not. And I'm not hungry either, although I need to partake of some food before the next contest."

"Well, I'm starved." The pixie polished off the food on her plate and went in search of more.

A novice jouster brought a jug to the table. He kept his eyes averted as he poured.

"Are you new?" Siv asked. "I haven't seen you before. Where are you from?"

"Slak. A small village in the western hemisphere."

Siv nodded. "I know it. How long have you been here?"

"I just arrived, Lady Siv." He bowed and walked toward the other jouster's table. He started to fill the cup and the beverage spilled across the stone tabletop. Altin leapt to his feet as the servant mopped with his apron.

Nyrin returned with a plate piled full of cakes and sweets. Between bites, she chattered, sometimes with her mouth full.

"I've talked to the other flight guards. Everyone is excited. Today is the day of reckoning. They've started a betting pool and you're favored to win." Nyrin polished off another cake. She inclined her head to the other diner. "Even Altin's guard bet on you. Only Dakrus and Rand's guards voted for their jouster."

"Hmmm." Distracted, Siv glanced around the room, trying to figure out what had caused a sudden disturbance in her mind.

A screech echoed across the room, and Altin

glanced at his scrying stone.

"I'm up first." The monitors displayed "SEMI-FINAL ROUNDS" and his name. The screen wavered until Rand's name appeared as his opponent. Under their names, the "Element of Afterlife" appeared as the banned art for the round.

He extended a hand. "You'll fight Dakrus then. Good luck, Siv. Defeat him. You'll make a good ruler."

"It's not over yet, Altin, but good luck to you, too." Never one with extreme hubris, Siv shook his hand. Altin headed out.

Siv said, "Let's go to staging, Nyrin."

"Almost ready." Nyrin grabbed her goblet and gulped.

"No!" Siv pivoted and knocked the cup to the floor. "How much did you drink?"

"The whole glass. Why?"

"Where is our server, the apprentice who brought the last jug?" Siv stomped up and down the aisles.

"I don't know. What is it, Siv?"

"There's something strange about him." Siv grabbed her temples and concentrated. Then she snapped her fingers. "He knocked the jug over at Altin's table but now I don't think it was an accident. It must be drugged. He poured me a glass but I never drank from it."

"It tasted fine to me. Let's go. We don't have a lot of time."

The two arrived at the staging area just as the gates closed behind Altin.

Ghy snorted a greeting. Siv gave her a reassuring pat. Her gaze drifted to the tub of water at the dragon's feet. Unease stirred in the pit of her stomach.

"Esrala, Giln!" Siv called the assistants. "Did Ghy drink this water? Where did it come from?"

"The cistern," they answered in unison.

"You're sure that's where it came from?"

"Yes," Giln said. "We drew it ourselves. Two imps carried a tub of water in, but they acted strangely.

Nasty little things. They began to argue and one pushed the other into the water. He was so dirty we chased them away and got fresh water for Ghy. I think they were high on something."

Siv slapped her forehead. "I should have realized there may be sabotage and kept closer watch." She glanced at the monitors as the scrying drones panned the scene. Thunderous applause railed through the speakers as Altin took his place. A mix of cheers and hisses greeted Rand.

"That drowd is getting guggly," Nyrin mumbled through puffed lips.

"What did you say?" Siv turned.

Nyrin's eyes rolled up and she fell forward onto her face.

Chaos ensued. An uneasy Ghy snorted puffs of gray smoke. The two apprentices bumped into each other, trying to help. Then Giln raced away to find a healer.

Heavy booing rattled the stadium. Siv stole a peek at the floating monitors. Rand had won the match and was on a short victory lap before returning to the West Stage.

"Nyrin, wake up! Wake up!" Siv cried. The pixie curled up and snored softly.

"We have to go without her, Ghy!"

The wyvern swooped low so Siv could climb onto the saddle. They blew through the gates to the starting point. Their opponents were already in the stadium, swooping and somersaulting. Dakrus' mount drifted to the starting point.

A new wave of cheers followed as Ghy lined up at the opposite end.

Siv's memory rings warned her that Dakrus aimed to dislodge her saddle. As he thundered down the field, he summoned fire to form a wall of flame and smoke, Siv called forth the blast of air she needed to keep her vision clear. She blocked his weapon with a mighty thrust from her shield. At the same time, Ghy twisted and slapped her massive tail into the chest of the opposing dragon, sending the beast and its rider crashing against a wall. Applause followed the two teams until they reached the end of the field and skidded around the U-turn mark.

With the next pass, Dakrus summoned the forces of death and the undead to surround him and his mount. Writhing, tortured souls formed a black wall of smoke, blocking him from Siv's view.

Lightning bolts flashed, sending shock waves throughout the stadium as Siv called on the elements of earth, air, and water. The strengths of the two powerful jousters brought them to a standstill as the arts warred against each other, stalled by some unseen wall between them.

Heat from Ghy's flaming breath propelled over Siv, whose clothing had already changed to the life-saving armor. She and Ghy both flapped their wings to further fan the air against the wall of godforsaken figures struggling to reach them.

Siv's memory rings warned her that the coronal had fallen off Dakrus' lance, revealing a sharpened metal tip aimed straight for her heart. Armor hardened over her. She stood in the stirrups and called forth the power of water. Her command of the combined arts was too much for Dakrus' power of death and the undead. The torrent broke through the invisible wall, engulfing the fiends.

Although thrown off balance by the flood, Dakrus' dragon continued the charge. Ghy careened her massive chest into the other dragon while Siv powered her lance at Dakrus' shoulder. The attack on his unbalanced frame sent him toppling from his saddle. He swayed at the end of the tether.

Derisive catcalls ensued. The umpire again declared Siv the winner. Tudoriax flipped his palm at Siv.

Dakrus' dragon began its flight of shame, circling the stadium until it could land the furious, dangling jouster onto a solid surface.

Ghy looped into one graceful somersault before flying to the staging area to thunderous approval from the crowds.

The five-minute intermission allowed just enough time for a comfort break.

After the monitors flashed Siv's and Rand's names,

scrambled letters flipped on the next line. At last, the letters fell into formation, revealing "ALL MAGICS BANNED."

The crowd roared in disapproval.

"Lady Siv! Can the council do that?" Giln cried.

Siv shrugged and mounted Ghy. "No telling what they can do, but this should be interesting." The duo headed onto the field.

The jousters squared off at their starting points. It was only then Siv realized that without magic, her armor would not form. Her memory rings remained dark.

As if reading her thoughts, Rand removed his armor. The spectators burst into cheers.

Rand was as handicapped as she—except as a Fire Elf, he never tethered to his saddle.

Determined to compete on an equal footing with her opponent. Siv stood in the stirrups and made a point of removing her tether. The crowd lapsed into silence.

Let this match begin. I'm ready.

On the first pass, Siv managed to slice one of the straps of Rand's stirrup. His lance snagged the billowy cloth of her sleeve. She jerked sideways, but remained seated. The dragons lashed at each other with their spiked tails and then continued to the opposite end with both riders upright.

The teams lined up for the second pass and charged ahead.

Siv stared down the padded coronal of Rand's advancing lance. She aimed hers, and in a microsecond, the two ends smashed together. The impact sent Rand's mount crashing against a railing while Ghy spun head over heels. Siv's coronal broke, leaving a sharp point.

Siv struggled to hold on. The crowd roared when Ghy righted and the feisty jouster still remained in the saddle.

Ghy steadied and rounded the U-turn, as did Rand's mount at the opposite end.

The next six seconds seemed to go by in slow motion. Siv raised her lance just enough to deflect

Rand's and she lunged forward. Her lance speared into his chest muscles straight through his scapula. Ghy's right wing struck him across the forehead. Her tail lashed out, sending Rand's dragon into a tailspin.

The impaled lance caused Rand to lose his balance. He slipped from the saddle, and began the fall toward the void. His dragon swooped to catch its rider.

For a second, Rand hesitated. With his injured arm, he caught the pommel just in time and heaved his body back into the saddle.

Despite the injury, he pulled himself upright. He guided his dragon on one flight around the jousting field with the lance still protruding from his body.

He met Siv in the center. "Your lance, Grand Sentinel, Ma'am." He pulled the spear from his shoulder and handed the bloody, broken shaft to Siv. He forced her hand upward to hold it aloft. The crowd went wild. A furious-looking Tudoriax gave a fling of his arm as he pointed to Siv and then stormed from the stadium.

Stomps and cheers rocked the arena.

"You're a worthy opponent, Siv," Rand said with a bow of his head. "Congratulations."

Siv's gaze drifted to the void below their feet, then to Rand's shoulder. "As are you, Rand. You should get your wound tended to as soon as possible."

"I will." Rand winked and let his gaze travel to the crystals on her suit. "If I come to you after the victory celebrations, will you wear this suit, if you can prevent it from turning into body-chewing armor?"

"Are you willing to take the risk?"

Rand paused and grinned. "Yes, I'll take that chance."

She smiled and said, "I'm glad you decided not to die your glorious death today. See you tonight." Siv nudged Ghy and the pair flew into their victory dance. Impressive bolts of lightning flashed silver and blue, winds blew away clouds to clear the sky. Misting water formed arcs of rainbows.

***

Ignoring the display of elements, Rand studied the amazing crystals covering Siv's form.

Some days, other things were more important than a glorious death.

ALSO BY ALLIE MARIE

THE TRUE COLORS SERIES

Teardrops of the Innocent: The White Diamond Story (Book 1)

Heart of Courage: The Red Ruby Story (Book 2)

Voice of the Just: The Blue Sapphire (Book 3)

Hands of the Healer: The Christmas Emerald (Book 4)

Child of Time: The Pearl Watch (Book 5)

HISTORICAL MYSTERY

Return to Afton Square

ANTHOLOGIES

"'TIS THE SEASON SWEET ROMANCE NOVELETTES"

It's a Wonderful Life After All

ABOUT THE AUTHOR

Award-winning author Allie Marie grew up in Virginia. Her favorite childhood pastime was reading Nancy Drew and Trixie Belden mysteries, never dreaming she would grow up to be a real-life sleuth with a career in national and international policing. When she embarked on a new vocation writing fiction after retiring from law enforcement, it would have been understandable if her first book was a crime story. However, researching her own family tree inspired her to write the True Colors Series instead. The other stories patiently wait for their turn.

Her debut novel, *Teardrops of the Innocent: The White Diamond Story*, was a 2015 New England Readers' Choice Award (NERCA) Finalist in paranormal. The second in the series, *Heart of Courage: The Red Ruby Story* earned two "Best Book" awards at the 2017 Indie Romance Convention Awards. The fourth book, *Hands of the Healer: The Christmas Emerald*, garnered a 2019 Rocky Mountain Best Cover Award as well as finalizing in the 2019 NERCA. The final book *Child of Time* released in 2019.

New books include *Return to Afton Square*, a WW1 historical mystery that is a sequel to the first series and a prequel to True Spirits Trilogy, a spin-off of her original series coming in winter 2021.

Besides family, her passions are travel and camping with her husband Jack.

Made in the USA
Middletown, DE
08 October 2022

12065887R00044